Bubbe's Belated Bat Mitzvah

Text copyright © 2014 by Isabel Pinson
Illustrations copyright © 2014 by Lerner Publishing Group, Inc.

KAR-BEN PUBLISHING
A division of Lerner Publishing Group, Inc.
241 First Avenue North
Minneapolis, MN 55401 USA
1-800-4-KARBEN

Website address: www.karben.com

Main body text set in Fink Roman 17/24.
Typeface provided by House Industries.

Library of Congress Cataloging-in-Publication Data

Pinson, Isabel.
    Bubbie's belated bat mitzvah / by Isabel Pinson ; illustrated by Valeria Cis.
      pages   cm
    Summary: With encouragement and Torah lessons from her
great-granddaughter, Bubbie has a bat mitzvah.
    ISBN 978–1–4677–1949–0 (lib. bdg. : alk. paper)
    ISBN 978–1–4677–4668–7 (eBook)
    [1. Bat mitzvah—Fiction. 2. Great-grandmothers—Fiction.]
I. Cis, Valeria, illustrator. II. Title.
PZ7.P6348Bu 2014
[E]—dc23   2013022209

Manufactured in the United States of America
1 – DP – 7/15/14

Bubbe's Belated Bat Mitzvah

Isabel Pinson

illustrated by Valeria Cis

KAR-BEN
PUBLISHING

"How many kippot have you made?" I ask Bubbe, as she hands me a crochet hook. "I bet it's a gazillion. You've done them for every Bar and Bat Mitzvah and wedding in the family."

Usually I go home after soccer practice on Sundays, but today my mom dropped me off at Bubbe's apartment. Bubbe is my great-grandmother, and she's teaching me to crochet.

"I've lost count," Bubbe answers, "but the first one I made was for my brother Charlie's Bar Mitzvah. He studied a whole year with the rabbi so he could read from the Torah. On Shabbat, when he finished reading his portion, everyone tossed candies at him to wish him a sweet life."

"Did you make kippot for your own Bat Mitzvah?" I ask.

"I didn't have a Bat Mitzvah, Naomi. When I was growing up, girls didn't study Hebrew and weren't called to the Torah. I was always sorry I missed that."

That night I think about everything Bubbe told me.

I dream that she is standing on the bimah reading from the Torah.

The next Sunday, Bubbe teaches me how to use different colored yarns for crocheting. "Did Grandma Rachel have a Bat Mitzvah?" I ask.

"When your grandma was growing up, girls still didn't read from the Torah, but for her Bat Mitzvah she was allowed to give a speech in the synagogue. She told the story of Moses and the Ten Commandments on Mt. Sinai. I remember every word. I was so proud of her."

"Bubbe, I think you should have a Bat Mitzvah," I say. "You'd be great!"

That night Bubbe ponders Naomi's idea.
She dreams that she is standing on the bimah, the Torah scroll open in front of her.

The next time I visit Bubbe, it's the week before Purim, and Bubbe and I are making hamantaschen. While we're cutting out the circles, I ask her to tell me about my mommy's Bat Mitzvah.

"When your mommy was 13, girls were reading from the Torah. She studied hard with the rabbi, just like Uncle Charlie, and we were so proud of her."

"You know Bubbe," I say, "you can read Yiddish.
The Hebrew letters are the same. You can learn to read Torah.
I really think you should have a Bat Mitzvah."

"But I'm 95, Naomi!" She giggles at the idea.

"You'd be awesome!" I say. "Let's ask the rabbi."

"You'll have to help me practice," Bubbe warns.

That night Bubbe and I have the same dream again.

On Shabbat after services, Bubbe and I talk to the rabbi. He is excited and encourages Bubbe to start studying. Now every Tuesday Bubbe goes to a Torah reading class. And every other Sunday mom drops me off at her apartment after soccer so I can help her practice.

We sit at the big dining room table, which is covered with a lacy white cloth. Our books are open in front of us. "What's this word again, Naomi?" she asks, and I remind her.

"Don't worry, Bubbe. You're getting better every week."

When Bubbe and I feel she is ready, we go back to the rabbi and set a date.

The next time I visit, Bubbe's dining room table is filled with books, notepads, and pencils. "The rabbi says I have to give a speech," she tells me. "It's been 75 years since I wrote an essay, Naomi."

"Abby can help you," I offer. My cousin Abby loves to write.

All of Bubbe's great-grandchildren want to help, so I assign them tasks. Noah is designing the invitation on his computer, and Natalie is addressing the envelopes. They can do this all the way out in California.

Nate is making a beautiful Torah pointer from beads. Samantha and Sasha are wrapping chocolate kisses in little squares of green fabric, Bubbe's favorite color. Ethan and Jacob are decorating baskets for the candy. I, of course, am crocheting kippot.

On the day of the Bat Mitzvah, our whole family sits together. I am right next to Bubbe.

When it's time for her to be called to the Torah, she squeezes my hand. "I'm so nervous," she whispers.

"Don't worry, Bubbe," I assure her. "Just read the way you read for me."

The cantor calls Bubbe's name, and she carefully walks to the bimah.
My cousins tiptoe among the seats handing out candy packets.

Bubbe picks up the Torah pointer. She looks up and smiles at me. Then she says the blessings and chants her portion, slowly and loudly so everyone can hear.

When she sings the last words of the blessings, everyone shouts "mazel tov" and showers Bubbe with candy.

As she walks back to her seat, everyone reaches out to shake her hand and congratulate her. I give her the biggest hug and kiss. "You did it, Bubbe, and you were awesome!"

"You were the best helper ever," she says. "And this is just for you."
She reaches into her pocket and hands me a silver crocheted kippah
with my name written in Hebrew. "We'll need more of these soon," she
says.

"And we'll both have to practice," I warn her, "because you'll have to
read Torah again – at my Bat Mitzvah."

This story was inspired by the author's mother, Esther Silverman, who became a Bat Mitzvah in 2012 at age 95.

She celebrated with all of her children, grandchildren, and seven great-grandchildren.

ISABEL PINSON is a librarian at the Goldsmith Early Childhood Education Center in Baltimore, Maryland. She is married and has two grown daughters. This is her first children's book.

VALERIA CIS was born and raised in Rosario, Argentina, where she still lives with her little son and her husband. She studied fine art at The University of Humanities and Arts in Rosario. She has illustrated many children's books including *A Tale of Two Seders* (Kar-Ben).